MOUNTAIN
OF FIRE

MOUNTAIN OF FIRE

The Daring Rescue From Mount St. Helens

PAUL THOMSEN

INSTITUTE FOR CREATION RESEARCH

SANTEE, CALIFORNIA

Unless otherwise noted, all Scripture quotations are from the New King James Version of the Bible, © 1979, 1980, 1982, 1984 by Thomas Nelson Inc., Nashville, Tennessee, and are used by permission.

Illustrations by Brian Thompson

Institute for Creation Research
P.O. Box 2667
El Cajon, California 92021
1 (800) 628-7640

Library of Congress Cataloging in Publication Data

Thomsen, Paul M., 1938—
    Mountain of fire / Paul M. Thomsen.—2nd ed.
        p. cm.—(Creation adventure series)
    Summary: Following the eruption of Mount St. Helens, two National Guard helicopter pilots make several dangerous rescue missions and uncover the mysteries of God's creation.
    ISBN 0-932766-44-7
    1. Rescue work—Fiction.   2. St. Helens, Mount (Wash.)—
    Eruption, 1980—Fiction. 3. Volcanoes—Fiction. 4. Christian life—Fiction.]
    1. Title. 11. Series
    PZ7.T37375Mo 1990
    [Fic]—dc20
                                         97-070389
                                           CIP
                                         AC

JFON
MMPPK

CHAPTER 1

The majestic stag elk shoveled the fresh, five-inch snow away with his massive head, uncovering the rich spring grasses beneath. For an instant he froze, his sensitive ears picking up a far-off sound from the valley below. Slowly raising his regal head topped by six-foot antlers, he scented the early dawn air; giant jets of steam hissed from his nostrils into the chill.

Looking over the mist-filled glen, his keen eyes searched the deep shadows of the spruce forest and beyond to the distant river valley where a dog barked sharply over the rumble of the Toutle River. That meant that man was in the valley. A dozen cow elk and their yearlings rose, stretching their necks above the mist, focusing their eyes on the majestic stag. A young buck moved close to the stag and stood at his side. Not a muscle moved. Silence filled the glen. Satisfied that danger was far-off, the stag lowered his mighty neck and resumed feeding.

Suddenly every fiber of his twelve-hundred-pound body tensed. Inches below his muzzle the very earth began to tremble. A low rumble echoed from the peaks thousands of feet above, and needles began to fall as the 150-foot fir trees swayed ever so slightly. Fear gripped this giant of the mountain. In an instant the entire herd bolted through the mist-filled glen, dashing at full speed into the deep shadows of the spruce forest. Driven by a sense of foreboding danger, the herd thundered through lush highland meadows, kicking geysers of sparkling water into the clear blue sky as it charged across Coldwater Creek.

With sides heaving, they slowed to a single gait under the hot noonday sun. Pausing briefly, the stag mounted a grassy knoll to survey the incomparable beauty of his domain—hundreds of thousands of acres of giant Douglas fir trees, pristine glacial lakes, streams teeming with steelhead trout, valleys

*Pausing briefly, the stag mounted a grassy knoll
to survey the incomparable beauty of his domain.*

of lush grasses—stretched before him on the north side of the mountain. As far as he could see, this magnificent land had been his. Virtually untouched, this wilderness was a perfect blend of nature in all its royal beauty. For ten seasons he had fought bloody battles to become the dominant beast of this land; and now, fighting his desire to stay, it was his duty to leave the valley of his youth, the domain of his conquests, and lead the herd from danger.

Pawing the ground with his huge foreleg, in one motion the powerful stag wheeled and bounded over a fallen log, followed by the young buck and the herd. On through the afternoon they kept the pace, on toward the other side of the mountain. Later, as the golden setting sun reflected off the crystal-clear lake, the herd waded out knee-deep to slack their immense thirst. These giant elk of the mountain, called wapiti by the Shawnee Indians, drank deeply from Spirit Lake. Medicine men, who once lived in lodges along its shores, claimed that on certain moonlit nights moanings could be heard coming from its depths, moanings from the spirits of long-dead braves giving warning of imminent danger.

The placid water rippled as deep underneath the earth trembled once more, sending the herd crashing to shore and off again on its fast-paced quest. As the night wore on, it was joined by hundreds of other wapiti in a migration of a thousand shadows gliding through the midnight darkness of the spruce forest. High on the mountain above them the moon revealed a slowly rising steam cloud venting from the volcano's cone. Dawn found the exhausted herd breaking the forest into a valley meadow along the shores of Pine Creek. All eyes fastened on the royal stag who stood looking back over his heaving shoulders toward the mountain. Slowly he turned his mighty antlers around and lowered his head to the dew-covered grasses. In total exhaustion, one-by-one the cows, yearlings, and the young buck dropped to their front knees, then sank beneath the soft mist. Only the stag remained standing as the first rays of dawn streaked through the treetops. Peace came to the herd— it was on the south side of the mountain.

ಶಿ   ಶಿ   ಶಿ

One hundred miles east of the herd and Mount St. Helens, fifty pilots of the 116th

Armored Cavalry Attack Helicopter Troop were gathering in the briefing room at the Yakima firing range. All were battle-hardened veterans, having served their country with distinction and valor in Vietnam. In the tradition of the minutemen who defended these United States with their muskets 250 years before, these pilots and crews were on constant alert and kept their skills honed razor-sharp by consistent training. They stood ready to defend their country on an instant's notice. With patriotic pride they saluted the American flag and pledged to defend its citizens against any enemy or any disaster that might befall—with their very lives they made this pledge. As dawn broke on this Sunday morning, the pilots were mustering at the briefing shack for their first day of gunnery practice. Captain Mike Cairns set his helmet and flight bag on the ready table, then squeezing his way past a row of battle-dressed men, he dropped into an empty seat next to his copilot gunner, Fred Phillips.

These men were rugged outdoorsmen as well as pilots—Mike Cairns in particular. He had, by the account of his fellow pilots, fished about every stream, walked almost every hiking trail, and slept under the stars of that mountain countless times. Combined with hundreds of flights around Mount St. Helens and its surrounding territory, he knew it about as well as any man who ever set foot on it. Like the old-timers before him, he was a mountain man—knowing every cliff, tree, and stream, and fully capable of living off the land if need be.

Captain Edelbrock entered the ready room. "All right, men, listen up." Fifty pairs of eyes fastened on the captain and the wall map behind him as he launched into the preflight briefing. "The ground crews are mounting your rocket pods now," he said, leaning on the edge of a steel desk. Then, just as he was about to launch into the briefing, the door opened and a red-faced first sergeant leaned in.

"'Scuse me, sir. There's an emergency phone call for you. I've patched it through—you can pick up on the desk phone next to you."

Captain Edelbrock picked up, then, listening intently, his face turned red and he stood ramrod straight. "Yes, sir . . . I understand, sir . . . immediately, sir!" Slamming the phone to its cradle, he looked up at the men. His lips tightened as his hands clenched the map pointer. "Men, the mountain just blew its top!" Every man snapped bolt upright. "It's the big one! According to my information, the explosion happened just minutes ago and went toward the north. First reports have it there is total devastation going out at least fifteen miles. Our immediate orders are to get all possible helicopters airborne, fly north out of range of the ash cloud, then west to Ft. Lewis where you'll refuel, then on to Kelso where you'll get individual orders for search and rescue. It's tough to tell if anyone could be alive in the blast area, but it's our duty to find out. The ash cloud is reported heading our way. It's only been thirty minutes, and it's up to forty thousand feet already. Get your aircraft preflighted and hold for tower clearance to take off. Let's scramble!"

Fifty battle-ready men bolted for the door, grabbing their flight bags and helmets off the ready table as they raced by. Outside, dashing down the runway, each man in turn was

"All right, men, listen up."

stunned by the pitch-black cloud coming at him, looming from horizon to horizon. Wild bolts of lightning crisscrossed the rolling, thundering mass. The doors to the Huey attack helicopter with 495 on its side were open. Mike and Fred leaped past the ground crew who were clawing at the release mechanisms for the rocket pods. Mike slid into his seat, pulled his shoulder harness on, and began his preflight. Fred poked him and pointed to the windshield. The sky had turned from brilliant blue to ominous gray-black. Bits of ash were already pinging off the Plexiglass.

From their left, down the tarmac, came a racing Captain Edelbrock. He was spinning his finger in the dust-laden air and yelling to each Huey as he raced by, "Don't wait for tower—light fire and get outta here! Go! Go! Go!"

Mike set the throttle and hit the starter switch. The low whine of the powerful turbine engine increased in velocity as the big forty-foot blades began to slowly turn. The instruments jumped to life. Faster and faster whipped the big blades till they became a blur.

"We've got sixty-six hundred rpm's, Mike," said Fred over the intercom.

Fifty battle-ready men bolted for the door.

Mike radioed the tower, "This is Guard Four-Niner-Five. We're departing runway zero-three-zero." Leaning out the door, Mike got a "thumbs up" from his ground crew who were running crouched over for the hangars. Moving the cyclic handle forward from the neutral position, he lifted Four-Niner-Five into the rapidly blackening sky. Of the twenty-five attack helicopters, only twelve made it off the ground before ash and bucking winds closed in, forcing the others to abort their takeoffs.

Five minutes out, at two thousand feet, Mike lost sight of the ground. He was now flying on instruments. Radioing the tower, he reported, "This is Four-Niner-Five. We're starting to get moderate to severe turbulence and heavy ash." Once . . . twice, his altimeter dropped two hundred feet. Each time the mighty blades fought for air, clawing to regain altitude. Pea-size ash rattled off the steel airframe. His hands began to sweat; blackness filled the cabin. Only the red glow of the instrument panel gave light. Lightning flashed once, then twice more, the bolts blazing across the windscreen. Tension and anxiety filled the blackness of the cabin as

Fred and Mike fought the heaving helicopter for control. Mike began to pray, "Lord, You're going to have to hold this thing together. Give us Your strength now. I put my life in Your hands." An inner sense of confidence came over him.

Lightning bolts streaked up at them from the blackness below, reminding Mike of his last raid in Vietnam that started him on that road to putting his trust in God and accepting Jesus as his Savior—his personal Savior. His thoughts flashed back to that midnight as the two attack Cobra helicopters streaked across the Vietnamese sky. It was hot that night; sweat ran down his chest, soaking his armored vest, or as his gunner, Paul, sitting in front of him called it, his "chicken plate." Their objective was to make a rocket run on enemy troops concentrated on the northern edge of a rice paddy deep in the U Menh Forest—"The Forest of Darkness." They were part of the 235th Armored Helicopter Company, nicknamed the Delta Devils. His Cobra was named Satan 15; his wingman flying next to him was in Satan 11.

From fifteen hundred feet his wingman rolled in first, commencing his run and firing rockets in pairs as he dove. Brilliant rocket flashes streaked to the edge of the rice paddy, exploding in a crescendo of orange. His 7.62-millimeter machine gun blazed, sending out a ribbon of red tracer bullets. On the pull out, his grenade launcher leveled the forest edge in a series of brilliant blue flashes.

"Satan 11, I'm rolling in to cover you." Mike peeled off on his rocket run, gaining speed to 160 knots. The enemy had come alive, and from his right, fifty-caliber machine-gun fire streaked up at Satan 15. At a distance the tracer shells looked like burning orange basketballs blazing skyward. He dropped down to a tree-skimming fifteen feet. His gunner up front leaned forward, fixing his eyes through the telescopic sights. Reaching forward with both hands, he squeezed the firing mechanisms. The Cobra shook as four thousand rounds in sixty seconds blasted the enemy. Mike squeezed off rockets in pairs. With a mighty *whoosh!* they screamed out, jolting the Cobra violently. From his left, AK47 tracers opened up, filling the air in front with green streaks. The blackness had come alive with green, red, and orange flashes.

His gunner yelled, "Break right, break right!" just as two AK47 tracers smashed through the Cobra windshield. The first shell crashed between the two men; the second tore through the gunner's armpit just under his armored vest, ripping his chest and left lung and blasting out his back in an explosion of steel and flesh, and then buried itself in Mike's instrument panel. The impact threw the gunner back, then he slumped forward, head and arms hanging limp from his shoulder straps.

"Paul! Paul!" No answer over the intercom. Mike radioed his wingman, "Satan 11, my gunner's been hit."

Just then, *wham! wham!* Two more AK47 blazing tracers smashed the cockpit window. Mike broke hard right—too late! A third enemy bullet smashed the window just as he flinched his head back a fraction—an ear-shattering explosion and his face shield literally blew apart. The tracer had impacted on the left side of his helmet, creased around his forehead, and blew out the right side. Intuitively, his left hand flew to his face; the shattered visor had blinded his left eye, leaving deep gashes across his face. He cleared his right eye of blood; then pulling pitch, the Cobra leaped skyward. Mike radioed his wingman, "We're receiving heavy fire—my front seat took a round through his chest, and I took one in the head. He's out, and I've lost my instruments."

"Roger, Satan 15. I'll drop down alongside you and show my lights. Command control has cleared us to a forward medical unit. Let's keep it low to minimize blood loss from air pressure." Through the blackness the two Cobras skimmed the snake- and enemy-infested jungle in a desperate race with death.

"Lord, I've never trusted You; now I've got to. Please guide this soldier home." Mike could taste a mixture of blood and sweat; the smell of burnt flesh filled the cockpit, and his gunner lay slumped over. For an eternal forty-five minutes Lieutenant Cairns fought fatigue, blood loss, and excruciating pain, all the while tracking his wingman with his one good eye. Then, out of the pitch-black jungle, a blaze of lights suddenly flashed on, illuminating a helicopter pad and a team of waiting medics beside it. He shot his approach, dropping the black Cobra onto its skids with a crunch, immediately killing the engine. Crouched-over medics came running under the blades with stretchers as

Mike popped his canopy. Reaching in front, he pulled the quick-release latch on his gunner's harness. Pulling him back, he could see the breath of life was still in him. They lifted Paul onto a stretcher and hustled for the operating room. Shrugging off the stretcher, Mike had time to reflect as he limped to the aid station, shattered helmet in hand. God had saved him—there was just no other explanation. For some reason He had spared this soldier.

As the doctors began to stitch up his battered face, Mike asked the medics how his gunner was doing. "He's critically wounded, but thanks to you, he's gonna make it!" Mike found himself doing something he had never done before in his life—he thanked God. The lights went out in Vietnam.

Suddenly the lights blazed in all their brilliance as the Huey broke from under the ash cloud on the north side of Mount St. Helens. Swinging around, both men were gripped in awe. The massive, black volcanic cloud in all its fury was boiling up to sixty thousand feet above them. The north side of the mountain was entirely engulfed. Lightning streaked everywhere; huge boulders as big as houses burst from the flaming, billowing ash cloud and flew thousands of feet through the sky. Spirit Lake, the Toutle River, Coldwater Creek, and the Green River—all of them had literally disappeared beneath the black devastation. Neither man could speak as they witnessed the awesome power of the erupting volcano. What death and destruction would lay under that mass of swirling black ash could not be imagined. All they knew was that they would be the first to find out.

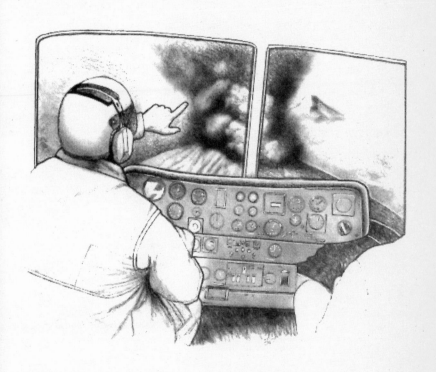

Neither man could speak as they witnessed the awesome power of the erupting volcano.

CHAPTER 2

Twelve hundred miles to the south, a long-tailed lizard sat on the edge of a flat rock basking in the 110-degree sun. His left eye looked down the gravel road toward the Indian village of Tuweep, while his right eye scanned the other way through the shimmering heat waves toward the north rim of the Grand Canyon. He caught sight of a dust cloud being kicked up by a distant, streaking red object. Becoming anxious, he began pumping up and down as his tongue flashed out, picking up vibrations of the now fast-closing object. As he became more excited, his skin began to change to the color of the gray rock on which he crouched, giving him a perfect camouflage.

The driver of the open-top, red Jeep leaned into the searing desert air, scanning the lava rock outcrop paralleling the desert road a hundred yards out. His teeth ground grit, and streaks of sweat ran across his forehead from under his Australian bush hat. Pulling hard right and slamming on the brakes, he threw gravel out fifty feet as he skidded to a stop. The lizard scurried under his protective rock.

The motor chugged roughly, rattling a bent fender on "Old Red" as the sunburned driver stood up on his seat to look over the reeds and mesquite that stood between him and the lava outcrop. Pushing back his hat, he raised dusty field glasses to his squinting eyes. The back of his shirt was soaked down to his khaki hiking shorts. Dropping his field glasses to his chest, he pulled a crumpled map out of his shirt pocket; then raising a leg up, he placed a battered hiking boot on the dash while unfolding the sweat-soaked paper on his knee. He took a stub of pencil out from behind his ear, glanced up at the rocks, then down to his map where he made an X. Grimacing into the sun, he smiled. "That's gotta be it!" Licking his cracked lips, he kicked his feet out from under him and dropped into the bucket seat. Only a geologist could become excited about finding a hunk of black lava rock, but this was his meat. Resting his chin between his hands on the steering wheel, he took a breather.

Steve Austin wasn't your typical Ph.D. geologist. This muscular ex-Navy officer worked the classroom all right, but his heart was in the field. He liked things that were massive and quick-happening, like floods and volcanoes—what textbooks call cataclysmic events, forces that caused dramatic geologic change quickly. Doing his undergraduate work at the University of Washington gave him the perfect opportunity to study the nearby volcanic range. One volcano in particular drew his interest and developed his expertise—Mount St. Helens—and he became an expert on it. The incomparable beauty of its forested slopes served as his base camp for many climbs to its summit. Setting out past the Toutle River flowage area, on up through the spruce forest, past the tree line, up the steep cone he'd climb and then descend into the hot, steaming crater itself to monitor listening devices set up by the U. S. Geological Survey crews—devices that felt the very pulse of the forces pushing from the earth's core deep beneath, building pressure, moving up to an imminent eruption. It would happen all right, and soon. In the evenings, back at the campfire on the shores of Spirit Lake, he plotted his strategy of observing his volcano before, during, and after the coming eruption. Somehow he felt by observing this cataclysmic event, he could uncover the secrets of the forces necessary to produce the geologic formations seen today, and perhaps unlock the ultimate question—the Creation itself.

At Pennsylvania State University he had earned his doctorate in geology. Back then, before he became a Christian, he considered himself an evolutionist, hearing his professors proclaim the fact that the earth is billions of years old and that by chance, through small changes over vast periods of time, the land formations seen today had come about. "We can prove evolution by radiometric dating volcanic rock, which gives us billions of years of age. We can see slow changes by looking at the Colorado River, which obviously dug the great Grand Canyon. It had to take millions of years, as that little river started out on top and cut down through the earth layer by layer, carrying away the sandstone grain by grain."

Once Steve got out of the classroom, he began his quest into the field; and it was there, out where the action was, that he began to generate serious questions about the theory of evolution. He went to the source—the Grand Canyon. Here there were volcanoes that had spilled lava over the lip, down to the canyon floor, giving rocks to date. Here was a massive canyon that somehow had formed, but what he found astounded him. Looking at a map of Utah, Nevada, and Arizona, he tracked the course of the Colorado River. It ran south from the mountains of Utah and then cut due west across Arizona, running from the right side of his map to the left. However, a giant land rise, the Kaibab Upwarp, goes from top to bottom, cutting smack across the river. In fact, that massive uplifting of the land would have made an insurmountable barrier for the river to cross over—a mammoth dam.

He remembered the words of an old miner he met on the Upwarp during one of his expeditions. "Sonny," he said, "I ain't no geologist, but any man can plainly see that in order for that old Colorado River startin' up here to cut a mile down through this here land uprise a little at a time over millions of years—well, sir, it woulda had to 'a flowed uphill; and every dagnabbed river I ever knowed flowed downhill. I ain't one to know how it happened, but one thing's sure—that tiny green river down there didn't cut this here canyon little by little the way them fellas from the Park Service say it did—just plumb couldn't 'a happened."

"Radiometric dating of the Grand Canyon volcanic rocks proves the bottom rocks to be millions of years older than the top rocks," his professors went on. But something about that stuck in Steve's craw. Evolutionists didn't use the same method to date the rocks on the top as they did to date the rocks on the bottom—something like comparing apples and oranges—yet no one ever questioned them.

Finally, how did all those sedimentary rock layers get put down in the first place? Sedimentary rock is formed by water picking up and depositing material, like sand or sea creatures, on the bottom in layers; and then under pressure, they harden. That's how sandstone, shale, and limestone are formed. Water had to have covered a huge area because some of those layers go clear across the United States. Only a massive deluge of water could have done that, like a flood—a world-covering flood. But none of his professors would admit to that possibility because it had biblical beliefs behind it, and they all agreed on one thing—God didn't do it. Evolution—it was void of God and riddled with holes.

All that was before Steve became a Christian. Then, one day he accepted Jesus as his Savior and made Him Lord of his life; he began to read the Bible, the only book God has ever written. It told a completely separate set of facts about creation versus evolution. He learned God created all things—including rocks, water, animals, and man—in six, twenty-four-hour days, no more than ten thousand years ago. He learned that through Adam's sin, death came on the earth. He learned that men walked away from God and became totally evil. He learned how God judged the earth with a catastrophic event—a world-covering flood—killing all land animals and all people except for Noah, his family, and two, or seven, of each kind of animal that were on the Ark. He learned how after a year, mountains rose, volcanoes erupted, and the waters rushed off the land.

The Flood—that's the key—that would have done it; that would have laid down those layers of sandstone, shale, and limestone in the canyon—a perfect explanation of why those layers go clear across the country. Then, as it says in Psalm 104, "The mountains rose and the waters ran off the land." That's when the Rocky Mountains to the north went up, and so did the Kaibab Upwarp, trapping a huge body of water between them. A gigantic lake formed across Arizona back to the mountains of Utah. Then, as the waters continued to accumulate, the dammed-up lake would have filled to the brim.

Then what? thought Steve. Pushing his Aussie bush hat back, he squeezed a clenched fist to his sweating forehead. "Let's see, the water would have overflowed the dam, cascading down the other side and creating a giant water-fall, and then flowed on to the lower land of California. As more and more water went over the Kaibab dam, the waterfall would have started to cut back into the dam—just like Niagara Falls is doing now—only it would have eaten backward faster 'cause the newly formed sedimentary rock would still be soft. The falls would have made a gorge through the still-soft sandstone toward the gigantic lake that fed it. Once it opened to the lake, the whole body of water would have come smashing through the gorge, exploding out the other side cutting the Grand Canyon. What would be left? A small river running down the path of the newly formed canyon. That would do it! The mystery of an uphill river would be solved. Now I've got to find out about that radiometric dating stuff!"

He threw "Old Red" into four-wheel drive, cranked the wheel right, slammed the pedal to the metal, and shot off toward the lava formation a couple hundred yards out. Through the mesquite and reeds, the old Jeep crunched over rocks, jolting from side to side, spitting gravel from all four tires, lurching forward— then *crunch! Well, close enough anyway*, thought Steve as he killed the engine and picked up his rock sledge and backpack. Just as he was swinging his left leg out, something told him to freeze. What was it? The only sounds were the tall hollow reeds rattling against the Jeep in the wind. Slowly he looked up. The sun blazed, sending shimmering heat waves and dust straight up off the hood of the steaming Jeep.

Wait! Straight up? There is no wind, but the rattling . . . Peering over his left shoulder, he slowly looked down, focusing on the dark, diamond-backed object only a foot from his boot and bare leg. It slithered back, coiling. The diamondback rattler raised, swaying his venomous head from side to side. Its forked tongue darted out, picking up the taste of Steve's sweating leg from the air. The viper's pits located and locked on its target by heat. His tail shook violently in a deadly buzz.

His body frozen, Steve's eyes locked on the snake. Out of the corner of his eye he caught another diamondback next to the tire. Yet another began to coil by the first, and another. *God, help me. . . . I'm in a nest of rattlers!* Now sweat poured down his forehead as his eyes held the slithering killers in frozen terror. Toxic venom buried deep in his leg by two-inch fangs from a five-foot diamondback rattler would mean certain, agonizing death.

His leg began to quiver with tension—it was now or never—more snakes were slithering out from the rocks. At lightning speed he yanked his leg up and slammed the door, clearing the deadly fangs. Firing the engine and grinding the gears in reverse, he rammed "Old Red" full

"God help me.... I'm in a nest of rattlers."

throttle backward, bouncing wildly as he careened to the road. Spinning around, he kicked gravel and headed back down the desert road toward his camp on the rim. Hitting the steering wheel with his fist, he shouted against the desert wind, "Man, . . . I hate those things. Those suckers really give me the willies!"

Back at his outpost camp that evening, Steve walked to the rim with a cup of coffee. Squatting down Indian fashion next to his campfire, he watched the spectacular color show as the rapidly setting sun played out a dazzling array of reds, purples, and blues against the layered Tapeats Sandstone, Kaibab Limestone, and Bright Angel Shale on the opposite canyon wall ten miles away. He picked up a small rock, looking at it while he sipped his coffee, and then tossed it out over the edge; five seconds went by before he heard a slight crack as his rock bounced off some object and continued its drop to the Colorado River flowing in the black depths more than a half-mile straight down—down to Lava Falls that looked like a small white strip on the green ribbon of water. "A lot of men have come here searching for answers to your mystery," he spoke softly to the chasm below. "I know I did, and I've found the answer—in the Bible."

Reaching over, he poked the fire with a stick, his eyes now transfixed on the dancing flames, brilliant against the desert sky. They reminded him of how the Bible spoke of God's coming judgment on earth by fire, and how men don't want to accept the fact that there is a God of judgment, and that's why they make up fables of how the canyon could have been formed without the Lord's hand doing it. They call it evolution by time and chance. The Bible affirms otherwise. No chance—God did it. No vast time needed—it's the result of His Flood. This canyon was a perfect witness to God's judgment on men by water. The very souls of those who perished testified to the curse of the canyon. But the Bible also says that God made a provision to escape His coming judgment by fire—acceptance of His free gift of salvation by believing in His Son, Jesus Christ, and making Him Lord of your life.

A kangaroo rat hopped past Steve, stopped, sat on his hind legs, and looked up at him with his big, soft eyes reflecting the flickering firelight. Then he scurried down his hole under a prickly pear cactus. Steve took another sip of coffee and listened to the absolute quiet of the canyon—the *big still* he called it. A full orange moon began to creep up over the far-distant canyon rim, looking massive in the chilly, clear desert air. Standing, he tossed the last coffee drops out of his tin cup onto the red coals. Then, shaking out his sleeping bag to make sure he wasn't sharing it with any desert critters, he crawled in. Laying back, he folded his hands behind his head and stared at the star-blazed sky. *Pure science—that's the key—that's what I need to confirm my belief in how the canyon was formed by a flood. Somehow I need to witness this event happening—observable evidence proves a theory.* His thoughts drifted back to Mount St. Helens, that majestic mountain he had lived with all those years—the awesome, cataclysmic power that lay beneath—the stuff that makes changes quickly. Could that mighty mountain hold the key? With that he drifted off, listening to the lonesome howl of a coyote echo through the canyon.

CHAPTER 3

The twelve Huey helicopters swung in and shot their approach to Kelso. As Mike settled Four-Niner-Five to a smooth touchdown, the refueling crews rushed out. Jumping from the cockpit, Mike ran over to the command control officer for his search-and-rescue orders.

"All right, here it is fast from the hip, Captain Cairns. There was a major earthquake at 8:32 this morning measuring 5.1 on the Richter scale. That triggered a landslide that peeled off a good chunk of the north face of the mountain. With the cork popped, all the pressure of the magma blasted up; and when the super-hot water and gases trapped in the magma hit the surface, they flashed to steam. That blast went off with a force of twenty million tons of TNT, or about two thousand atomic bombs, and blew the whole top of the north side right off— blasted it out over a 150-square-mile area. That's been followed by pyroclastic flows of vaporized pumice, earth, and gases goin' out at two hundred miles per hour, reaching 800 degrees ten miles down the valley—well over a 1000 degrees closer to the blast zone.

"Don't fool yourselves that it's over, though, 'cause that sucker continues to go off with the power of one A-bomb every second. No one has ever flown in, around, or under one of these things in a helicopter, and we have no idea what to expect. I can only tell you this—expect the worst, 'cause you can bet you'll bloody well get it.

"Now we've got reports of campers in the Green River region and the North Fork of the Toutle River—that's gonna be your search-and-rescue area. It's our duty as National Guard soldiers to be the first to respond to disaster, and you'll be the first helicopter in. We'll be in constant radio and radar contact from command control. Now crank your ship and go! And, oh yeah . . . God be with you, Captain!" With a terse salute, the major wheeled and made for the other incoming Hueys.

Mike, Fred, and their crew raced back to Four-Niner-Five. Strapping in, Mike looked up. He could see the massive billows of the exploding volcano rising to sixty-five thousand feet. "Nobody has ever done this before, Fred. We'd better do some serious prayin' 'cause things are gonna get pretty hairy!" Fred knew Mike's background in Vietnam and the decorations he had been awarded for valor, having been shot out of the sky three times—twice at night. His captain was made of steel—proven under fire—but most of all he knew of Mike's absolute faith and trust in Jesus Christ. If he had to go into a gutsy situation, this was the guy he'd choose to follow. As the mighty turbine began to whine and the big blades started to spin, Mike said over the intercom, "Guard Four-Niner-Five is lifting for search and rescue."

As they entered the blast zone, base control's radio crackled to life. "This is Four-Niner-Five. We're down to less than a hundred feet visibility. I'm slow flying at about fifty feet—if I go any lower, I kick up ash and it's a total blackout. For some reason my turbine isn't sucking ash—must be the blades are downwashing the intake clear. This is really grotesque up here. Every tree is down—the bark is blasted clean off. We've gone over thousands of them—look like scattered toothpicks. In some areas it appears the ground is still shaking, and there's steam vents shooting up all over—ash covers everything. We're getting violent bursts of hot wind vortices along with wild bolts of static electricity—it's tough to maintain level flight. Our inside temperature has passed 120 degrees, and we're still twelve miles out from the blast epicenter. This is supposed to be where the Toutle River was, and I don't recognize a thing—it's just plain gone. We're lookin' at hell on earth!"

Fred poked Mike and pointed out at three o'clock. He swung the Huey's nose around and edged close to the gray object appearing under the ash a hundred feet out. "Control, we've got something here—appears to be a pickup truck. The tires are melted and the paint's all seared off. We're closing in. I can make out somebody slumped over a log behind the pickup. Now I can see a form inside the cab—looks like the driver's hands are still on the steering wheel as if he were trying to get the truck moving and

*. . . a father's last desperate attempt
to save the life of his family.*

make a run for it." Then Mike and Fred spotted the boy at the same time. He was lying in the back of the pickup, face up. Both pilots choked, their battle-hardened eyes moistened as they hovered fifty feet above, looking on the frozen sight of a father's last desperate attempt to save the life of his family. "Base, we've got a young boy in the back of the pickup—appears to be about ten-years-old."

"Roger, Four-Niner-Five. Any life?"

For a second Mike couldn't respond, then choking, he stammered, "He's lookin' right up at me, base. Negative life."

For hours Mike and Fred crept over devastation. Edging ever closer to the blast zone, the Huey shook and shuddered in the violent wind shifts, lightning bolts, and exploding steam geysers. On they flew over boulders and glacier ice blocks bigger than houses tossed out ten miles from the exploding cone. Their searching eyes burned with the heat, sulfur gases, and ash—all mixed with sweat pouring down their bodies in the intense cabin heat.

"Base, I'm moving up to what's supposed to be the North Fork of the Toutle River, but it just isn't here. All I've got is ash, mud, downed trees . . ." Mike's voice choked off as Fred grabbed his arm in a steel grip. There in front came a massive wall of mud cascading straight at them. "Pull up, pull up!" By just feet, the seventy-five-foot-high mass of mud, ash, boulders, and hundred-foot trees crashed wildly beneath them, churning the already-pulverized landscape. High on the mountainside, the super-hot volcanic ash and magma had made contact with surface and buried glacier ice, melting it instantly and sending a huge torrent of water roaring down the slopes. Two miles wide, the boiling tidal wave of mud shot past the hovering Four-Niner-Five and roared down the valley, decimating everything in its path.

Mike radioed Captain Stebner in *396* further down the valley. "Darrell, a massive mud wave shot by us. Watch it, it's gotta be seventy-five feet high, and it's movin'!"

"Roger, Four-Niner-Five, it's already past us. We clocked it goin' at better than fifty miles per hour way down here. Now we're on the back side of the mud flow—what a mess! Don't see how anything could make it through this. Hang on, there's a huge tree . . . and, yeah . . . there's a body hangin' on the root ball." Captain Stebner maneuvered for a closer look. Then from the body a desperate arm raised slightly. Darrell yelled over the radio, "Mike, the guy's alive!"

Captain Stebner studied the situation. There was scalding hot mud on either side, the wind was gusting badly, wild bolts of lightning were slashing, and visibility was down to fifty feet at times. If he went in, he'd have to barely touch that log, keeping pace with it as it slowly oozed along, and make certain the skids didn't contact the mud, which would instantly suck in the Huey. "The odds are stacked against us," he told his crew, "but we're going in. Open the port-side door and prepare for rescue." Slowly, gingerly, he maneuvered his craft, hovering inches above the muck-oozing tree. A National Guard doctor serving as crewman hung out the door, feet on the skids, motioning for the man to crawl the ten feet across the log toward him. Hesitantly, the logger let go of his death grip on the roots, got down on all fours, and began to crawl forward. Now the crew could see his badly burned face; his blackened, shredded clothes whipped in the prop wash. The roar of the turbine drowned out his desperate cry for help through blistered lips.

Hand over hand he crawled toward the outstretched arm of the crewman. Halfway to the hovering Huey his grip slipped, the logger's already charred hand going down into the hot mud. Pain gripped his face as he lifted his mud-caked arm out toward his rescuers. Then a half-inch bolt of static electricity shot across from the logger's outstretched fingertip to the extended fingers of the doctor! *Wham!* The blue bolt blew the doctor back through the open door, across the cabin, smashing him against the other cabin door. The impact lifted the Huey slightly. The logger dropped facedown on the log, arms sliding back into the mud as he hugged the trunk.

Although stunned, the doctor got to his feet and motioned Captain Stebner to maneuver for another try. With steeled nerves and steady hands, he again hovered, this time to within inches. They could see the desperate, terror-filled face of the logger as he once more reached out with a blackened arm pleading for help. "Come on, come on, you can do it," screamed the crew over the engine roar. Inch by inch he crawled; then leaning out as far as the doctor possibly could, their hands locked. "We got 'im; we got 'im! Pull up!" shouted the crew as they slid the logger through the door. Captain Stebner lifted just as the tree rolled over in the bubbling muck.

"What's your position, Darrell?" radioed Mike from Four-Niner-Five.

"We got our guy off the log. I'm headin' for base. Good huntin', Mike."

By sixteen-thirty military time (4:30 p.m.), hundreds of survivors had been plucked by the hovering Guard helicopters from the lower valleys, some snatched from the claws of death, clinging desperately to the very tops of 150-foot trees that showed a scant ten feet above the rising mud. But for Captain Cairns and his crew further up the mountain, closer to the blast zone, it was a different story. For six hours they had fought the volcano that still erupted with a force of one A-bomb every second. By now their sweat-soaked bodies were caked with ash, their eyes tearing from the gases, teeth grinding with grit. Hours before they had passed the fatigue barrier, being driven on now by super-human strength—God's strength. Yet, as they came upon victim after victim, anguish slashed at their hearts. For Mike and his crew, there was only death on the mountain. Still they pressed on in their desperate search for life as

"We got 'im; we got 'im! Pull up!"

the ashen air got even darker in the late afternoon. Following a logging road that bordered a sheer rock cliff, Mike kept Four-Niner-Five facing the rock ledge, slowly maneuvering the Huey sideways up the log-strewn road.

Then, "Wait! Hang on, Mike!" shouted the crew chief. "Over there at your two o'clock position—I think I saw something red flash."

Mike swung Four-Niner-Five slightly to the right. Through the chin bubble he could see nothing but swirling, boiling ash. Edging a bit farther, he lowered to thirty feet. "There, I see it again. Mike, look at that; it's a guy waving in a red plaid shirt." Fighting to hold the Huey in the hot, blasting wind shifts, Mike edged even closer, his skids just clearing the jumbled mass of downed trees, his blades a scant fifty feet from the sheer rock edge of the canyon wall. "I can see three of them now. One guy's waving, and there are two more stumbling 'side of him. We got live ones, Mike. Live ones!" Adrenaline pumped into the veins of the exhausted crew, snapping them into an excited frenzy of expectation. This is what they had waited for—a chance at life, a chance to defeat the death-dealing mountain!

"I got 'em, I got 'em now," said Mike, sitting ramrod-straight and holding Four-Niner-Five as close to the rock ledge as he dared. "We'll have to back down the road a piece and find a place to set down. Too many trees and junk here." Edging sideways, Mike backed Four-Niner-Five down the road, keeping his eyes fixed straight out on the rock ledge now only thirty feet from the big spinning blades. Beneath them tangled trees and rocks were strewn across the smashed road; jets of steam shot up between them. Slowly, he backed down, his tail pointing out over the sheer drop-off.

The logging road made a U-turn around the outside of the cliff. "There's our spot, Fred," said Mike through gritting teeth. The yellow caution light flashed—low fuel—the tension mounted on their sweating faces. Neither man said it, but they knew now they'd have one shot; there would be no "go-around." Mike would have to plant the skids on the very edge of the road, tail hanging out over the drop-off. Ten feet too close and the blades would impact the rock; a foot too far back and Four-Niner-Five would careen backward into the black depths of the drop-off.

"I'll have to come nose in with our tail hangin' out in space, eyeball it, lower the pitch, and quickly land before the prop wash causes a blackout from the ash." A blast of hot gases pushed Four-Niner-Five back; the road disappeared in an ash cloud. Edging forward, they caught sight of the cliffside road again. The big blades reverberated in an ear-shattering scream off the rock ledge a scant twenty feet away. Every shred of his being concentrated on the landing target. "Lord, this is it—You take over now." Taking a deep breath, Mike shot the approach, and Four-Niner-Five dropped hard with a crunch. Ash and gravel flew off the road into the black abyss. The Huey teetered on the brink and then settled solid. Hissing air from his lungs, Mike said, "We did it! Thank God!"

The crew chief was already out the door as Mike broke open his harness; clambering out his door, he ran around to meet him at the nose of Four-Niner-Five. Looking up, they could see less than ten feet of air between the big blades and the rock cliff. They grinned at each other, white teeth flashing through black-ash faces; then charging knee-deep through ash and dodging steam blasts, they pushed up the road. Through

*The Huey teetered on the brink
and then settled solid.*

tearing eyes they stared into the depths as they hugged the wall and sidestepped a cave-in. Then clambering over jumbled logs, they both stopped, listening with cocked ears. Above the howl of hot, blasting air and the roar of the exploding volcano, they heard a faint cry, "Over here, over here." Through the swirling ash came three smoldering shadows groping through knee-deep ash; falling, getting up, and stumbling on—on toward the drop-off!

"Don't move. Stop!" Mike shouted. "The ledge, the ledge . . ." Bolting over the last log, the rescuers ran to the trio.

"Oh, thank God. Thank God!" gasped a young woman as Mike lifted her to her feet.

What clothes were on them smoldered, black soot covered their faces, their eyebrows and lashes were seared off, and the soles of their shoes had melted. Swooping the woman's arm over his shoulder, Mike led the desperate group back down the road. Over the jumbled logs they clawed. Hands in a vice grip, Mike yelled in her ear, "Don't look down!" as they edged past the drop-off with their backs to the jagged rock ledge. On down the logging trail they stumbled. Her legs collapsed—the girl hung in

Mike's arms. He pleaded, then commanded, "You can make it—just a few feet to the bend in the road! God, give us strength now." Once again they stumbled on, fighting total exhaustion, choking in the ash-laden air. Then out of the swirling ash and venting steam blasts appeared Four-Niner-Five, her chin sticking defiantly at the mountain, her tail proudly bearing the American flag, jutting out over the precipice. Never had Four-Niner-Five looked so beautiful, thought Mike, as he helped lift in the trio and climbed through the cabin door, collapsing in the cockpit.

"Four-Niner-Five, can you read me? Do you copy, Mike? We've been trying to raise you," called base.

Lifting the radio to his black, sweat-streaked face, Mike reported, "Four-Niner-Five is back with you, base. We're headin' home—we got live cargo this time!"

For six days Captain Cairns and his fellow National Guard pilots and crews forged into the swirling, exploding blast area. Sleeping beside their helicopters on the tarmac at night, rising before dawn, lifting off at first light into the incredible elements, they performed hundreds of heroic rescues. As the weeks wore on, the mighty volcano gradually spent its fury, sending an ash cloud that circled the entire world. Still, the pilots and crews of the National Guard searched the carnage for the remains of those caught in its aftermath. A huge new crater remained where the eruption had blasted off the old mountaintop, and unseasonably heavy summer rains began to fill it. The deep fall and winter snows settled on the peaks, turning to water as they hit the still-hot rocks on the steep volcanic walls. Slowly, the new mile-wide lake filled with water, cooling, calming the giant's red lava heart.

CHAPTER 4

A lone shadow moved silently through the spruce forest. Dawn was hours away, but it would take all of that for the old wapiti to finish his trek to the north side of the mountain. His steps were slow now, slowed by bones grown weary over the seasons. No more was the stag followed by the herd; his flanks bore the deep scars of battle where he lost that place of honor to a young stag buck two winters before. Alone, with head drooping, he plodded on, driven by an inner sense to return to his former domain where he had fought for and won his position as dominant stag—back to the North Fork. No more did he bound over fallen trees; instead, he sought the soft ground around obstacles. On through the day he pushed his aged bulk till sunset when he cleared the forest on the north side of the mountain.

His hooves kicked up dry ash and his heaving lungs sucked in dust as the old wapiti labored up a rocky ledge overlooking the North Fork. He lifted his head and with tired eyes viewed his once-pristine domain. No more did the pure waters of the Toutle River cascade in a hundred small waterfalls to the valley below; it was buried under six hundred feet of landslide, ash, and mud. No more crystal-clear lakes teeming with trout—only muddy, backed-up waters filling the flowage behind the immense landslide dam. No more rich, majestic fir forest as far as the eye could see; rather, millions of the giants lay flattened, stripped of their bark, like fallen soldiers robbed of their armor. No more lush green meadows with their life-giving rich grasses— only cinders, craters, and gray ash. No more cry of the golden eagle in the blue sky high above, nor the chirping of the thrush in the dew-covered meadow. No more whisper of the wind through the dark green pines. The only sound was an occasional hiss from a steam vent that sent up a small geyser of ash across the barren landscape. Then silence . . . dead silence.

Once more the stag felt the earth tremor beneath him as he had three seasons before. This time the wapiti didn't show terror; rather, he raised his mighty head topped by battle-scarred antlers, turned, squared his haunches, and fixed his determined eyes on the steaming moonlit crater high above him. With all his regal splendor, the stag made his stand—his last stand. Another tremor sent a crack splitting down the volcanic cone high above him. A trickle of water broke through, forced by the immense pressure of the huge lake within the crater. Another tremor, more violent than the first, and with a sheering, grinding, rock-splitting roar, the crater burst open, spilling billions of gallons of muddy water down the mountain. Once more the valley shook with a roar as the cascade crashed into the dammed-up Toutle River basin.

For hours the waters flowed out of the crater and poured into the basin behind the landslide. Then, in the blackness of the midnight, the basin filled, and the waters spilled over the rim of the landslide dam in a waterfall. As more water flowed into the basin from the crater lake, more water rushed over the brim, creating an even greater waterfall, which began to cut back through the landslide, eating its way through the dam toward the water-filled basin. Through the night it continued to cut away the soft dam, creating a gorge until it dug itself back to the main basin. Then with one final burst, the waters of the backed-up basin were released and exploded through the gorge, cutting a wider canyon on the other side before slowing and flowing to the valley below. As the sun rose over the volcanic cone, only a small creek trickled down the basin, through the gorge and the canyon, and on to the Toutle River far below. Once again silence blanketed the north slopes; once again there was death on the mountain!

ଯ   ଯ   ଯ

The phone jangled. Half asleep, knocking it off the cradle, an exhausted Steve Austin picked up, "Yeah, what's up?"

"Steve, this is John up in Portland. We had some good-sized quakes on the mountain last night. At sunrise the U. S. Geological Survey sent a plane up to shoot some photos of the north side. Hang on to your hat! It looks like the cone split last night, spilling the whole crater lake down to the dammed-up basin behind the Toutle River landslide."

Steve sat bolt upright in bed. "Yeah? Then what happened?"

"It's tough to tell from the photos—about all I can say is there appears to be some erosion through the landslide dam. We'll have to eyeball that for ourselves to verify. I can tell you this—the crater lake is almost empty! A ton 'a water went down that mountain! I've already cleared through the Forest Service for us to make our hike in on foot. We'll rendezvous at the crack of dawn tomorrow at base camp and then ride out to Spirit Lake where we'll head in on foot. Better hightail it on up here!"

Cradling the phone on his neck, Steve started pulling on his Levi's. "Did you get us a copter and pilot?"

"Yeah, I did. Got a guy from the National Guard. They say he knows the mountain about as good as anybody—rescued a bunch of people up there during the eruption three years ago."

"Great!" said Steve, pulling on a boot over his hiking sock. "Let's hope he doesn't have to drag us out! I'm on my way—should be in Portland by sundown." Dropping the phone, Steve grabbed his backpack, stuffed in an extra pair of socks, jumped in "Old Red," and said a quick prayer as he dashed for the San Diego airport, "Let this be it, Lord—may it be that key!"

At sunrise Steve met with his team. They helicoptered to a base camp on the edge of the spruce forest, landing next to the still-devastated blast zone. There they met a ham radio operator and a Forest Service ranger who would lead the group. The ranger laid out the operation. "I understand you want to inspect the new flowage basin and canyon formed by the crater lake washout. Well, this is how we're going to handle it—we'll start in together and then drop off our ham radio operator on high ground so he'll be able to maintain contact with Portland—those guys are constantly monitoring the seismographs looking for any tremors. As we continue, I'll drop off and be in contact with him by walkie-talkie while keeping eye contact with you geologists. If we get any indication from Portland that looks suspicious, my radio operator will raise me, and we'll call for the helicopter pickup immediately. I want it perfectly clear, you two guys, that we're going into extremely dangerous territory, and under no circumstances will we spend the night out there." Then looking square at the pilot, he continued, "If that mountain so much as burps, I'm calling you in fast! I want everyone on constant alert!"

The group drove to the shores of Spirit Lake. From there they proceeded cross-country on foot toward the flowage area. Single file they hiked, kicking dust from the six inches of ash that covered everything. Sinkholes and minicraters were everywhere. Their feet sweat profusely as heat permeated the soles of their boots from the still-hot cinders under the ash. No one spoke as the men trudged. Viewing the desolate aftermath, a hollow, sinking feeling of death filled each man. Even after three years there was no life. High on a ledge overlooking the drainage basin, they dropped off the radio operator who set up his equipment, stretching his big whip antenna skyward to bring in Portland.

As they got close to the erosion area, they came upon a side canyon, and the Forest Service ranger higher up waved his arm for the two geologists to continue. Sliding down on the jagged rocks, Steve crossed a creek. Reaching down to test the water, he yanked his hand back—it was scalding hot. A strange metallic odor filled his nostrils. He cupped his mouth and hollered across to John, "Follow your side of the gully down—I think it'll connect with the main drainage area." Waving, John turned to head down the side canyon, careful to stay clear of steam vents that erupted in mini-geysers along the side walls. On through the high-noon sun, the two men picked their way. The rocks were hot to touch as Steve reached out to balance himself around a crumbling ledge. "Watch it, John!" A huge chunk of the canyon wall gave way and crashed to the gully floor with a roar.

The dust and ash settled. "Steve, I can't make it any farther over here—I'm blocked. I'll have to cross over to your side," shouted John from across the creek bed, his voice echoing down the ravine. Pausing, he removed his sweat-soaked leather hat and poured water from his canteen over his sweating head. The cool water felt good running down his chin and chest. Clearing his eyes with thumb and forefinger, he searched for a crossover spot—a solid-appearing bridge of crusty rock over the creek. Gingerly sidestepping, he began to cross, holding his arms out to balance. One more step and suddenly the whole area turned to Jell-O. "Hang on, I'm going through!" His boots broke the outer crust; hot, quicksand muck underneath gripped his feet. "Steve, I'm being sucked in—quick, my legs are goin' in!"

"Fall on your back—I'll throw you the rope." Running as close as he dared, he tossed a rope to his struggling partner. Steve gave the rope a twist around his hand, threw it over his shoulder, grabbed the end with his other hand and pulled hard, leaning back with all his weight. Taking a deep breath, he heaved again, the rope biting into his shoulder and neck.

John lay flat on his back, arms stretched over his head, hands gripping the hemp rope. He winced in pain as the rope slipped his grip, burning his hands. Regripping, he yelled through clenched teeth, "Pull, man . . . pull!" Gradually the hot muck released its suction grip on one foot. Quickly he dug in his free heel and pushed. Gritting teeth, both men strained. With one more tandem heave, the other foot broke free. Hand over hand, Steve reeled John in, who skidded on his back across the crumbling rock bridge. Shaking, John stood. The two men fumbled to pour water from their canteens over John's blistering legs.

Then, standing back, Steve put his hands on his hips and asked his partner, "Well, what do ya' think? Wanta hang 'er up and head on back?"

Bending over, John picked up his hat and gave it a swat on a rock, knocking off hunks of mud. Smiling, he cocked his head and looked up, "And let you make the discovery all by yourself? We've waited three years for this day. No chance! Let's go get 'em!" The two men laughed, then Steve gave John a whack on the back as they started up the crumbling ravine toward the main objective—the breached landslide dam.

Lying flat, they belly-crawled the last ten feet toward the ledge. Then peering over, Steve gave a low whistle as they looked straight down into a 140-foot gorge. "Will you look at that!" Staring across at the sheer cliff before them, they could see multiple layers of strata. The evidence was perfect of how water had filled the basin off to their right, overflowed the landslide dam, and fell in a waterfall to their

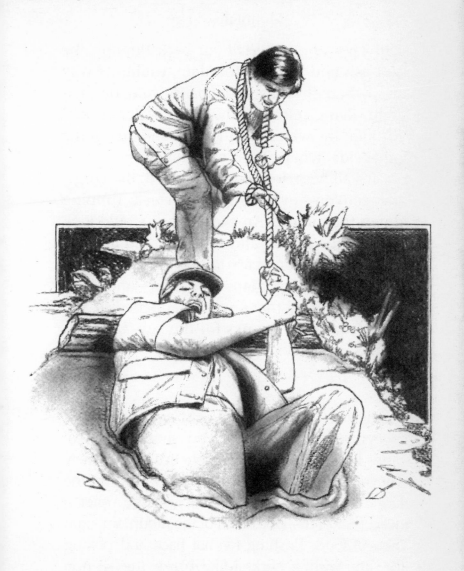

He winced in pain as the rope slipped his grip.

left. Then the waterfall cut back through the soft ash and mud of the dam, eating its way past where they lay to the basin water on their right. Being released, the basin water rushed through the waterfall-cut gorge and on out the other side, where it carved a canyon.

"It's all here, John—the lake bed, the gorge, the canyon—even the little creek running down the middle. An evolutionist would look at that little stream and say, 'That did it. Must 'a taken a million years to do!' We know for a fact it took less than six hours—and to a greater degree, that's what happened at the Grand Canyon! Thanks for the key, Lord . . . thanks for unlocking the mystery."

⚥   ⚥   ⚥

The crackling campfire sent sparks into the amber sunset sky; the placid shore waters of Spirit Lake reflected the silhouettes of two men. They squatted Indian fashion, eyes fixed on the flickering flames—one a geologist, the other a helicopter pilot—both men of the mountain, both men of God. Pushing his hat back and poking the fire with a stick, Mike broke the silence, "Something still gnaws at me, Steve—this radiometric dating stuff. I mean, don't these evolution guys date rocks at billions of years?"

Hesitating a second, Steve half-smiled, shook his head, and softly spoke at the flames, "Yeah, they do, but let me tell you about that. I collected thirteen samples from a lava flow that came out of volcanoes on top of the north rim of the Grand Canyon. The stuff actually went over the lip of the canyon, so it had to be the newest rock with all the layers underneath—sort of like the frosting on a cake. Then I got samples of rocks from way down at the bottom of the canyon, underneath all the other layers—they had to be the oldest. Anyway, I sent the samples to an evolutionist laboratory that dated them both with the rubidium-strontium isochron method—the most technically advanced system available. The results came back showing the rocks on top of the canyon, which had to have been the youngest, to be one billion years older than the rocks on the bottom. In my book that means that either the canyon is upside down, or the whole system of radiometric dating doesn't square. Either way, something's rotten in Denmark."

"What do you really believe happened out there, Steve?"

"The Bible says we have a sovereign God that judged the earth as the result of evil man and caused a world-covering flood several thousand years ago, and the aftermath of that flood formed the Grand Canyon. Through that judgment, He saved a remnant of animals and eight God-believing people to repopulate the earth. That's what the Bible says; that's what I believe."

Mike poked the fire again, sending another shower of sparks dancing into the now dark sky. "Ya' know, Steve, the Bible also says the Lord will return again to judge all people—like a thief in the night He will come, and some will be taken and some left. I saw an example of that up on the mountain, back when it was boilin' mad. That first afternoon I picked up two campers—they had been trout fishing with another couple and had their tents staked right next to each other. When the blast hit, they all dove into their tents. I found the one couple stumbling along a logging road later that day. We shot our approach and made the pickup. They were in pretty rough shape, but lived through it. Four days later, the parents of the other couple that were camped next to them met me at the airstrip at dawn. They asked if I'd please search out their kids, even though they feared the worst after four days of fire and brimstone up there.

"We flew in a small helicopter because we knew it would be tough landing among the mass of downed trees. The mountain was still venting its fury, but we managed to locate the two yellow tents—had to put down a mile away in a small clearing. We packed in chain saws, radio, and gear—took us two hours to fight our way over hundreds of jumbled logs. When we came upon the campsite, there was one tent still standing just the way it was pitched; not two feet away was the other, crushed under two huge trees. We spent the better part of the afternoon cutting, wedging, and blocking out the trees. When we finally freed the tent, I gently cut away the yellow rain flap. We pulled it back, and there was the young couple, their lifeless arms embracing each other—I tell you, that dropped us to our knees. Later, as an Air Force helicopter hoisted up the body bags and flew back down the valley, we just sorta stood there staring at the ground, arms hangin' down; our hearts were heavy with grief for those kids and for their parents waiting back at base. In that moment of reverence—just for a scant few minutes—the volcano quieted and all was absolutely still. I closed my eyes and said a silent prayer.

"Then, 'What was that?' Fred whispered. We froze—listened—nothing. 'Wait—there, I heard it again—over by those logs; listen.' Then we all heard it—a soft whimper. Up, over the logs we went. Sliding down the other side, we came up short. There, pinned under a downed tree, was a beautiful shepherd dog peering up at us with two of the biggest, prettiest brown eyes I've ever seen. 'It's the dog his dad talked about. It's Tie—their dog, Tie—and she's alive!' shouted Fred.

"We ran over to where she lay pinned, whimpering softly, her muzzle flat on the ground; and then our eyes beheld a scene we'll never forget. Right there in front of her nose were three puppies sort of snowbanked in with ash, pointing toward her. They obviously hadn't moved in four days—probably hadn't nursed either with their ma pinned under the log. We dropped to our knees and broke open our canteens, giving our last precious reserves to the pups and Tie, and then put the pups in a backpack and proceeded to block, wedge, and cut the log which was pinning old Tie. None of us really gave her much of a chance—figured her back was broken and in all probability we'd end up having to put her out of her misery. Gently, oh so gently, we lifted the blocked log off her back. To our delighted amazement, Tie jumped up, shook, and barked. Then the pups jumped out of the backpack, and all at once guys, pups, and old Tie were rolling on the ground—laughing, hugging, and kissing. I don't know who was happier—us or the dogs. I tell ya', we had tears and dog slobber all over our faces.

"Later that afternoon, I gently swung around to settle the helicopter back at base. As we approached, the red sunset cast long shadows off one pitiful sight. There was a small group of folks huddled together, and off to their left a few paces, over next to the Air Force helicopter, all alone knelt the father, head bowed over the body bag that contained his son. I shut down the engine and opened the cabin window. In the quietness of the evening, I could hear soft sobbing coming from the group. It was a heart-wrenching scene against that setting sun—one that will remain with me forever. I waited for a respectful minute or two, gathering my composure, and then opened the cabin door. Immediately Tie bounded out and made straight for the father. She ran right up and put her paws on the kneeling dad's shoulders, nuzzling his face and neck. The lad's father swung around and hugged Tie, rocking back and forth on his knees. Then the pups squirmed out of the backpack, plopped to the ground, and broke out into a run for the little group of people who swooped them into their arms.

"We got out of the helicopter and stood in the shadows, taking in the joyful, tearful reunion. After a moment, I walked over to the father who was still hugging Tie. I put my hand on his shoulder and said, 'I don't know why God chose to allow your son's friends to live and why He chose to take your boy home, but I do know we have a sovereign God, and through Him we'll find the comfort and strength to continue.'

"He hugged old Tie harder while stroking her head and neck. After a moment, he softly said, 'I want to thank you for bringing my boy back.' Then looking up at me with tears streaming down his cheeks, he continued, 'And I

"I do know we have a sovereign God, and through Him we'll find the strength to continue."

thank God for giving me a living remembrance of my son.' Tie whimpered and licked his face."

❧ ❧ ❧

The last flickering flames reflected off the moistened eyes of the two mountain men—these men of God—as they stared into the burning embers. A gentleness of spirit enveloped the campsite. Down in the valley, down in the dark spruce forest, a young wapiti stag raised his five-foot antlers to the rising full moon, stretched out his mighty neck, and called. The mellow notes echoed across the North Fork, and then drifted over the still waters of Spirit Lake. The herd was back, back to the north side of the mountain.

EPILOGUE

For action under fire during his 1969-70 tour of duty in Vietnam, Lieutenant Mike Cairns was awarded:

- The Distinguished Flying Cross
- Air Medal with "V" for Valor
- Purple Heart
- The Vietnamese Cross for Gallantry

For his heroic flying during the 1980 Mount St. Helens eruption, Captain Cairns received the Humanitarian Award from the State of Washington, which is the highest award for State service. He also received the Valley Forge Cross, which is the highest National Guard award for valor. Mike and his wife, Chris, have two children and currently reside in

Bellevue, Washington, where Mike is general manager of Register Tape Advertising, Inc.

      ಶ   ಶ   ಶ

Steve Austin received his bachelor of science in geology from the University of Washington in 1970, his master's degree in geology from San Jose State University in 1971, and his doctorate in geology from Pennsylvania State University in 1979. From there, he went on to the University of Colorado to study glacial geology on a National Science Foundation stipend. Dr. Austin has authored *Catastrophes in Earth History* and *Grand Canyon: Monument to the Flood* . He is currently chairman of the geology department at the Institute for Creation Research and resides in San Diego, California, with his wife, Brenda, and their two children.

ABOUT THE AUTHOR

Paul Thomsen graduated from the University of Wisconsin (Madison) in 1960. Through his career as an international executive and corporate owner, he has lived in and traveled much of the world.

Paul and his wife, Julie, have created Dynamic Genesis, Inc. and endeavor to produce books for the Creation Adventure Series of which *Mountain of Fire* is a part. They also conduct seminars for school students, teaching them to answer questions on origins the way the public school textbook presents them, and then "qualify" their answers with a nongradable, biblical, scientific answer. This "qualifier" system has received enthusiastic approval from both teachers and students.

The Thomsens have seven children and live on a small lake in northern Wisconsin.

While in the San Diego area, visit the

Institute for Creation Research

and its *exciting*

Museum of Creation and Earth History

10946 Woodside Avenue North
Santee, California 92071
or call for information at (619) 448-0900